Learning About Art

Heather Hammonds

Chapter 1

Our Art Show

Our class had an **art show** last week. Everyone made something for the show.

Lisa and I made a big **collage**.
Our collage was about our school.

Here is the teacher.

Here are the students.

Here is the school.

Kali painted a **portrait** of her new brother. She wanted everyone at the art show to see him.

Tim made a **sculpture** of his dad. He wanted everyone at the art show to see his big, strong dad.

Chapter 2

A Visit to the Art Gallery

Before our show, we went to see some **artwork** by other **artists**.

Our teacher took us to an **art gallery**.

The outside of the gallery is also a piece of art!

The art gallery was very big.
There was art inside the gallery.

There was art outside the gallery too.

Chapter 3

Paintings

Kali wanted to see some paintings.
She liked this portrait of a girl.
It looked a bit like a photo.

I liked this painting of a pond.
I liked the green colours in the painting.

Everyone had a favourite painting.

Chapter 4

Sculptures

Tim wanted to see some sculptures.

We saw sculptures that were made of:

- metal
- wood    
- and glass.

Some of the sculptures looked like people and animals.

Chapter 5

Old Art

We saw some very old art.

We saw sculptures that were made long ago and paintings that were hundreds of years old.

Long ago, there were no cameras.
People could not take photos.
So artists painted lots of portraits.

Today some artists still paint portraits.

Chapter 6

New Art

The art gallery was having a special art show.
We saw new paintings and sculptures.
We saw a collage too.
I liked the collage best of all.

The artist who made the artwork was at the gallery.
She talked to us about her art.

Chapter 7

Being a Part of Art

We saw an artist dressed up on a chair. He was being a part of his art.

The teacher told us that this kind of art is called **performance** art.

Chapter 8

Art Everywhere

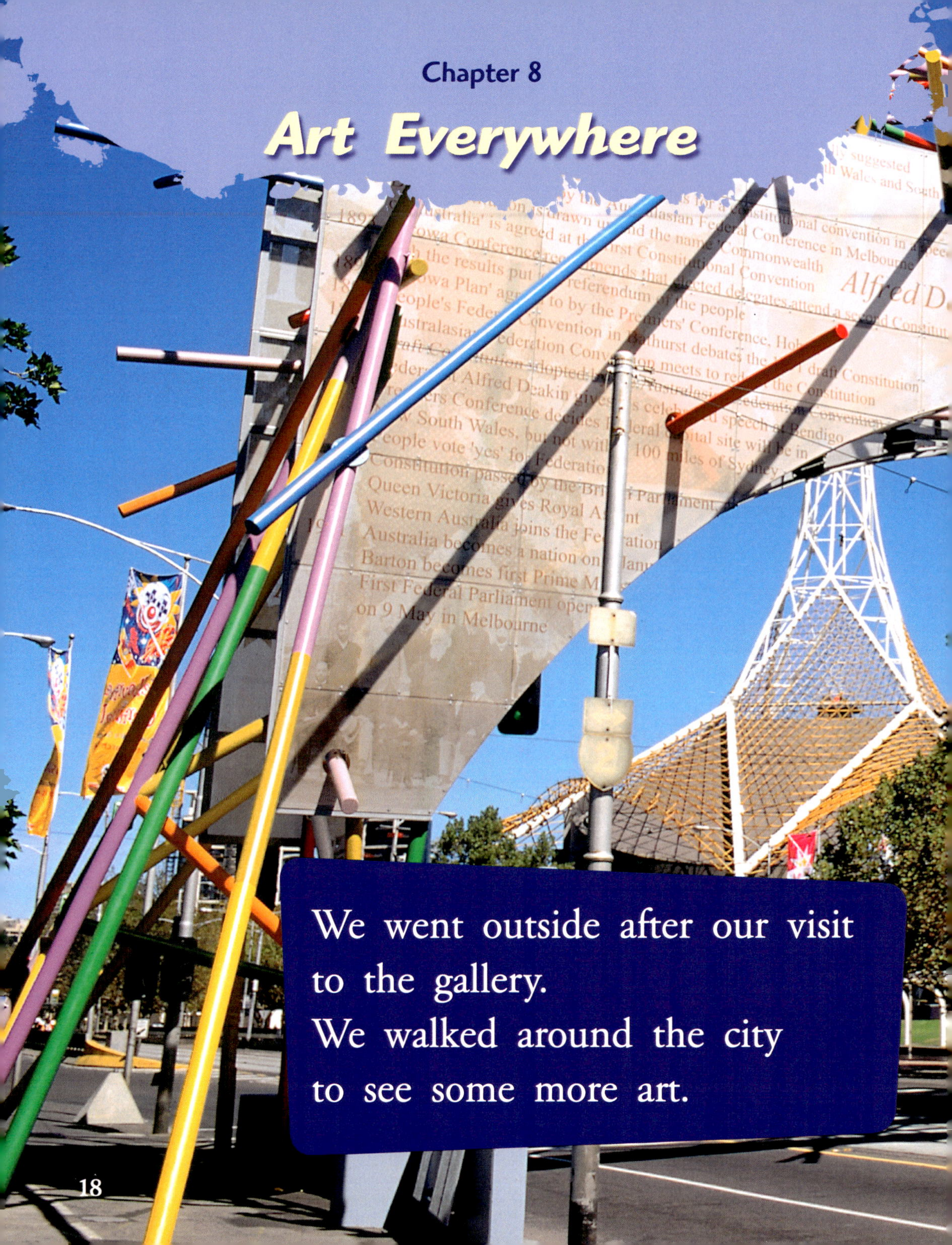

We went outside after our visit to the gallery.
We walked around the city to see some more art.

We saw a big **arch** with lots of coloured sticks.

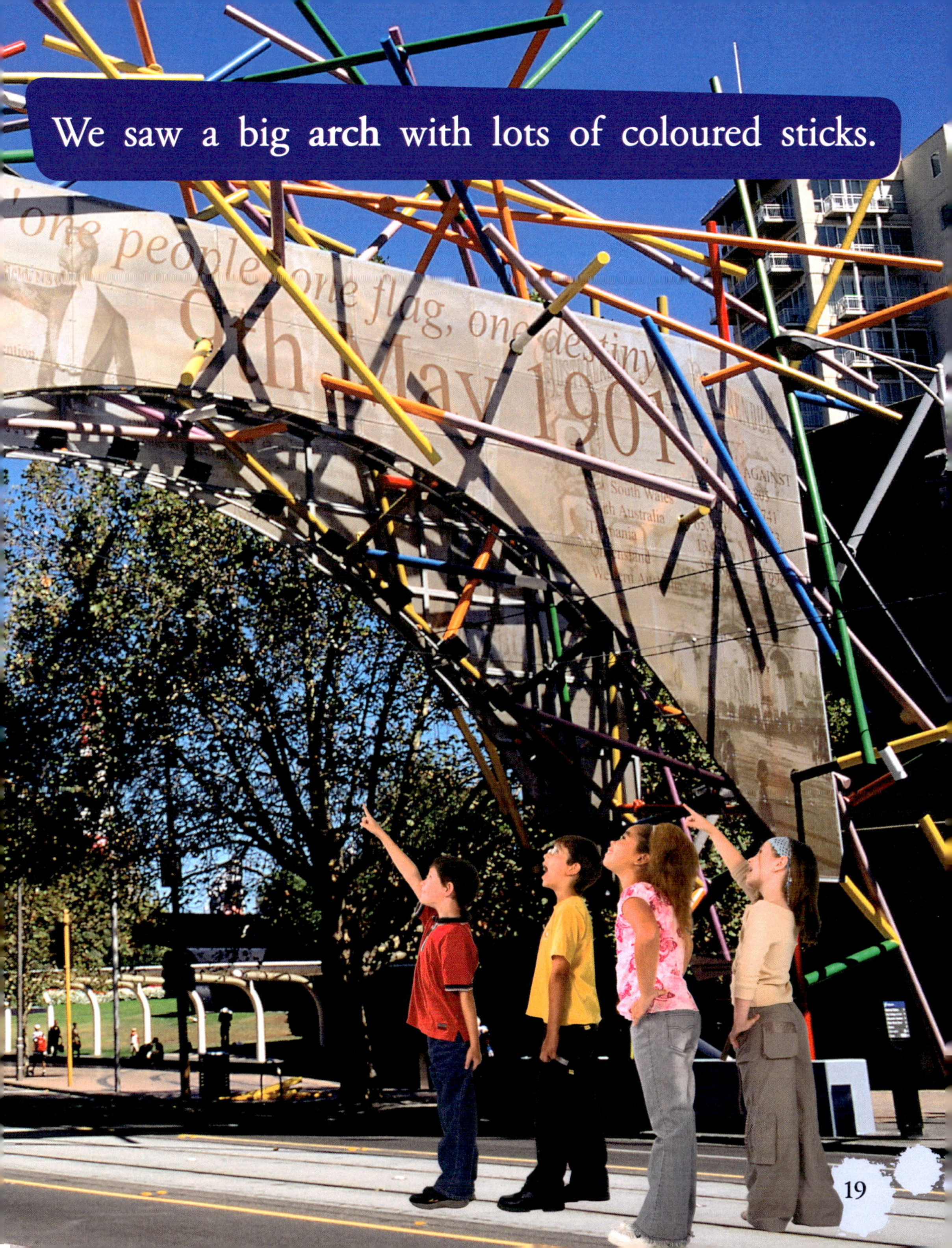

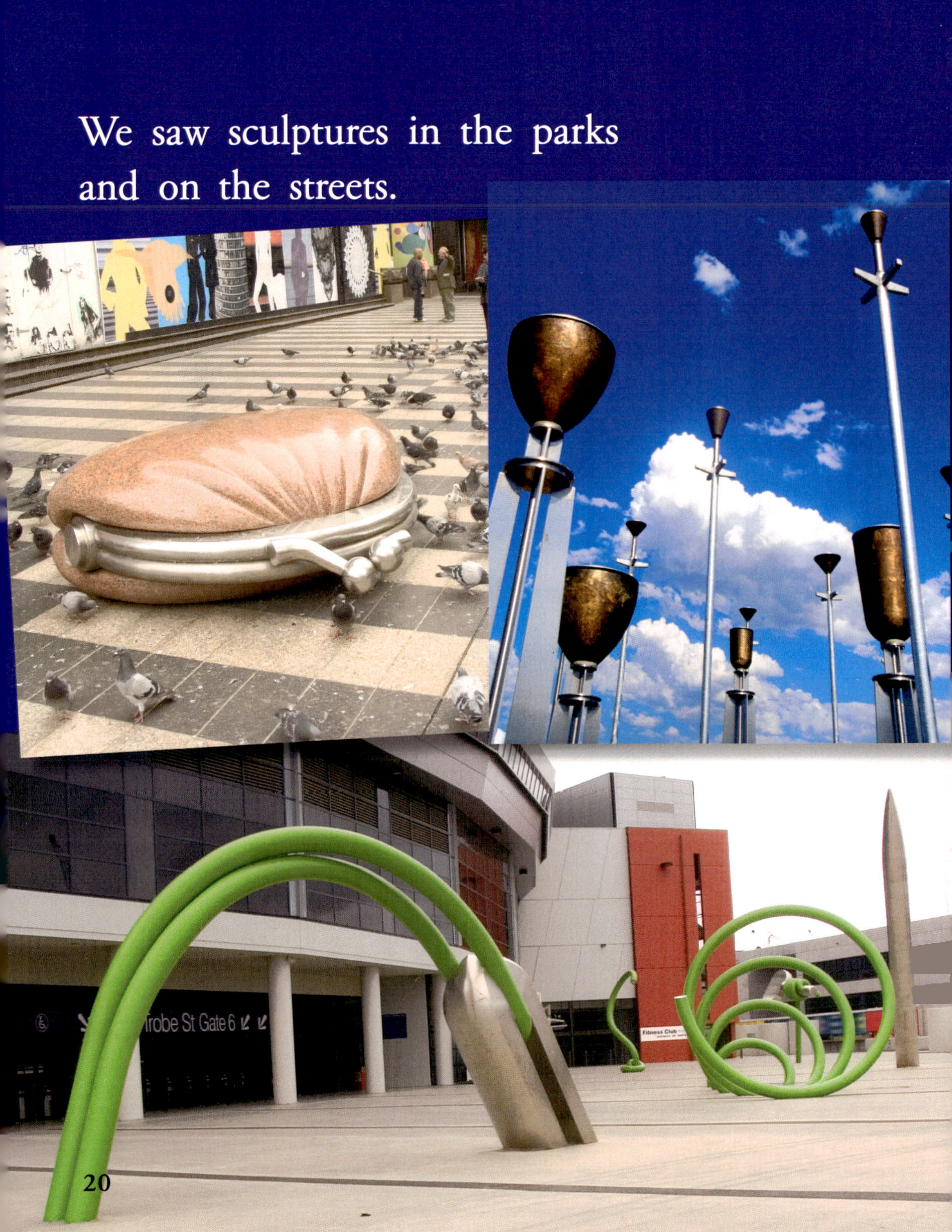

We saw sculptures in the parks and on the streets.

We saw some very old statues.
We saw some new statues too.

We even saw a big bird.

Chapter 9

Learning About Art

We learned a lot about art.

We learned that:

- There are lots of different kinds of art.
- Art can be made from different kinds of materials.

- Artists can be part of their art.
- Art can be seen inside and outside.

- We are very good artists too!

Glossary

arch a curved building or object that sometimes goes over the top of a road, bridge or footpath

art gallery a building where people go to see lots of artwork and art shows

art show a show where artists show the artwork they have made

artists people who do art

artwork art such as a painting or a sculpture

collage a piece of artwork made by putting different things like paper, cardboard and paint together, to make a picture

performance an act – something that is put on for an audience

portrait a picture of a person

sculpture a model, shape or figure made in art

Index